P9-DDG-901

GEORGE AND MARTHA ROUND AND ROUND

JAMES MARSHALL

HOUGHTON MIFFLIN COMPANY BOSTON

For My Mother

Library of Congress Cataloging-in-Publication Data

Marshall, James, 1942–

George and Martha 'round and 'round/James Marshall.

    p.   cm.

Summary: Five episodes chronicle the ups and downs of a special friendship.

    ISBN 0-395-46763-2

    {1. Friendship—Fiction. 2. Hippopotamus—Fiction.} I. Title.

PZ7.M35672Gee 1988   88-14739

[E]—dc19   CIP

                                     AC

Printed in the United States of America

RNF ISBN 0-395-46763-2

PAP ISBN 0-395-58410-8

WOZ   20 19 18 17 16 15 14 13

FIVE STORIES ABOUT THE BEST OF FRIENDS

STORY NUMBER ONE

THE CLOCK

George gave Martha a present
for her birthday.

"It's a cuckoo clock," said George.

"So I see," said Martha.

"It's nice and loud," said George.

"So I hear," said Martha.

"Do you like it?" asked George.

"Oh yes indeed," said Martha.
But to tell the truth,
the cuckoo clock got on Martha's nerves.

The next day

George went to Martha's house.

Martha was not at home.

And the cuckoo clock

was not on the wall.

"Maybe she likes it so much

she took it with her," said George.

Just then he heard a faint

"Cuckoo . . . cuckoo . . . cuckoo."

To George's surprise,

the cuckoo clock was at the bottom

of Martha's laundry basket.

When Martha returned,
she couldn't look George in the eye.
"It must have fallen in by mistake,"
she said. "I do hope it isn't broken."
"Not at all," said George.
"The paint isn't even chipped,
the clock works just dandy,
and the cuckoo hasn't lost
its splendid voice."

"Would you like to borrow it?"

asked Martha.

George was delighted.

He found just the right spot for it, too.

Wasn't that considerate of

Martha to lend me her clock? thought George.

"Cuckoo," said the clock.

George invited Martha

on an ocean cruise.

"Is *this* the boat?" said Martha.

"Use your imagination," said George.

"I'll try," said Martha.

Very soon it was raining cats and dogs.

"This is unpleasant," said Martha.

"Use your imagination," said George.

"Think of it as a thrilling storm

at sea."

"I'll try," said Martha.

"Lunch is served," said George.

And he gave Martha a soggy cracker.

Martha was not impressed.

"Use your imagination," said George.

"Oh looky," said Martha.

"What a pretty shark."

"A shark!" cried George.

George took a spill.

"But where's the shark?" he said.

"Really," said Martha.

"You must learn to use
your imagination."

STORY NUMBER THREE

THE ARTIST

George was painting in oils.

"That ocean doesn't look right," said Martha.

"Add some more blue.

And that sand looks all wrong.

Add a bit more yellow."

"Please," said George.

"Artists don't like interference."

But Martha just couldn't help herself.

"Those palm trees look funny," she said.

"That does it!" said George.

"See if you can do better!"

And he went off in a huff.

"My, my," said Martha.

"Some artists are *so* touchy."

And she began to make

a few little improvements.

When George returned
Martha proudly displayed the painting.
George was flabbergasted.
"You've ruined it!" he cried.
"I'm sorry you feel that way," said Martha.
"I like it."
Martha was one of those artists
who aren't a bit touchy.

STORY NUMBER FOUR

THE ATTIC

One cold and stormy night

George decided to peek into the attic.

"Go on up," said Martha.

"Oooh no," said George.

"There might be a ghost up there,

or a skeleton, or a vampire,

or maybe even some werewolves."

"Oooh goody!" said Martha.

"Let's investigate!"

But there wasn't much to see in the attic,

only a box of old rubber bands.

George was disappointed.

"Would you like to hear a story

that will give you goose bumps?" asked Martha.

"You bet," said George.

"When you hear it, your bones will go cold,"

said Martha.

"Oooh," said George.

"Your blood will curdle," said Martha.

"Ooooh," said George.

"And you'll feel mummy fingers

up and down your spine," said Martha.

"Stop!" cried George. "I can't take any more.

Tell me some other time!"

That night Martha went to bed
with the light on.
She had a bad case of goose bumps.

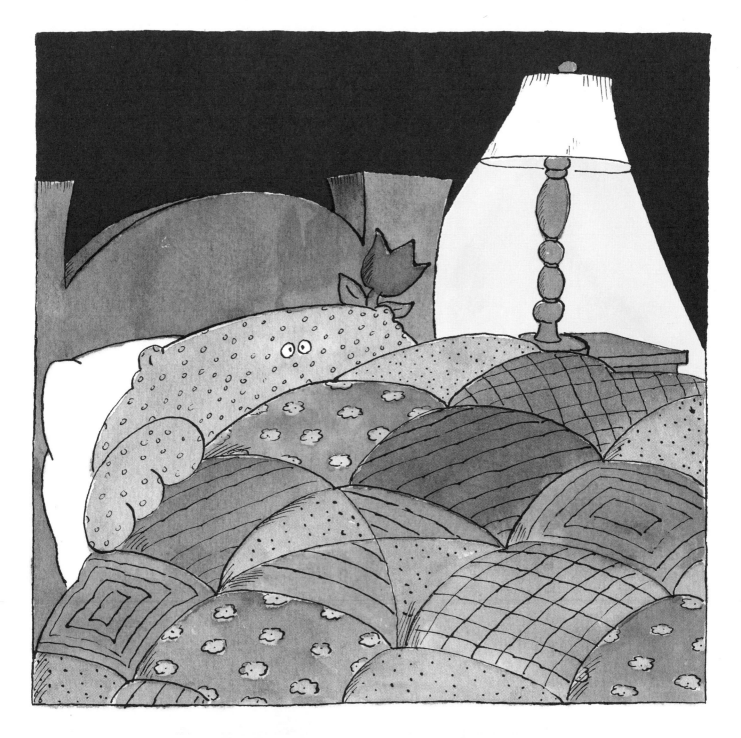

One late summer morning
George had a wicked idea.
"I shouldn't," he said.
"I really shouldn't."
But he just couldn't help himself.
"Here comes the rain!" he cried.
"Egads!" screamed Martha.

Martha was thoroughly drenched
and as mad as a wet hen.
"That did it!" she said.
"We are no longer on speaking terms!"
"I was only horsing around,"
said George.
But Martha was unmoved.

The next morning, Martha read a funny story.

"I can't wait to tell George," she said.

Then she remembered that she and George

were no longer on speaking terms.

Around noon Martha heard a joke on the radio.

"George will love this one," she said.

But she and George weren't speaking.

In the afternoon Martha observed

the first autumn leaf fall to the ground.

" Autumn is George's favorite season," she said.

Another leaf came swirling down.

"That does it," said Martha.

Martha went straight to George's house.

"I forgive you," she said.

George was delighted to be back
on speaking terms.

"Good friends just can't stay cross
for long," said George.

"You can say that again,"
said Martha.

And together they watched the
autumn arrive.

But when summer rolled around again,
Martha was ready and waiting.